The Fisherman
and the
Theefyspray

To Jack

With warm wishes

Paul Jennings

Thank you to Dr. John Coleman, Miki Wilson
and Cathy van Ee
- J.T.

Viking
Penguin Books Australia Ltd
487 Maroondah Highway, PO Box 257
Ringwood, Victoria 3134, Australia
Penguin Books Ltd, Harmondsworth, Middlesex, England
Viking Penguin, A Division of Penguin Books USA Inc.
375 Hudson Street, New York, New York 10014, USA
Penguin Books Canada Limited
10 Alcorn Avenue, Toronto, Ontario, Canada M4V 3B2
Penguin Books (N.Z.) Ltd
182-190 Wairau Road, Auckland 10, New Zealand

First published by Penguin Books Australia, 1994
1 3 5 7 9 10 8 6 4 2
Copyright © Paul Jennings, 1994
Illustrations Copyright © Jane Tanner, 1994

Typeset in Bembo
Made and printed in Australia by Southbank Book

National Library of Australia
Cataloguing-in-Publication data:

Jennings, Paul, 1943-

The Fisherman and the Theefyspray

ISBN 0 670 82972 2.

I. Tanner, Jane, II. Title.

A 823.3

The illustrations in this book were executed in
watercolour, gouache and coloured pencil.

PAUL JENNINGS

The Fisherman
and the
Theefyspray

— *Illustrations by* —

JANE TANNER

VIKING

Deep in the still cold shadows the last
Theefyspray looked out from her lonely lair.

There was not one other like her now.
Not in the heavens. Or the hills.
Or the deeps of the hushed green sea.

Starfish swarmed. Garfish gathered.
There were twos. And threes.
And thousands.

But the Theefyspray swam alone.

Then at the sunlit end
of one solitary afternoon,

a pain grew and flowered,
deep inside her.

Now there were two Theefysprays.

They hunted together, mother and child.

The baby was always hungry…

Up went the little Theefyspray.
Up where no fish should go.

She filled the sea with her silent scream
until every fin fluttered in fear.

Up went the mother...

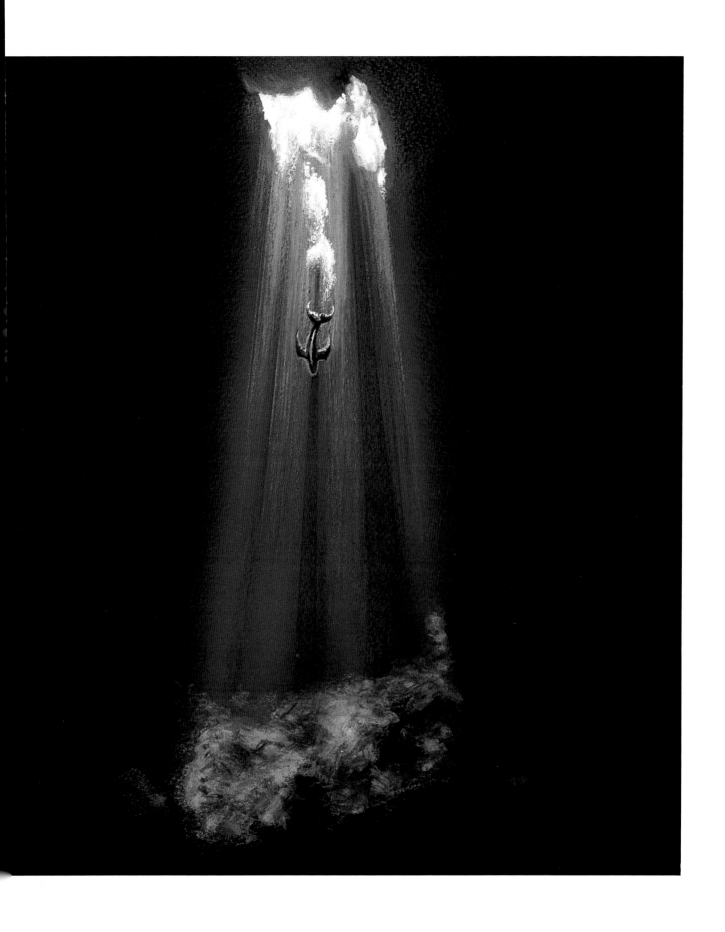

The mother sank slowly into the empty sea.

The fisherman had never seen
a Theefyspray before.

He wanted to show this strange,
beautiful creature to his friends.

But as he watched, the baby's colours
bled away in the sunlight.

The old man felt sad. Sorry. Ashamed.
He remembered the mother's shining scales
and flashing fins.

He put the Theefyspray back.

And went home with an empty basket…

…and memories.